Firelight Secrets

STORY BY **EDEL WIGNELL**

ILLUSTRATIONS BY **SUSY BOYER**

PM Chapter Books
part of the Rigby PM Collection

U.S. edition © 2001 Rigby
a division of Reed Elsevier Inc.
1000 Hart Road
Barrington, IL 60010-2627
www.rigby.com

06 05 04 03 02
10 9 8 7 6 5 4 3 2

Firelight Secrets
ISBN 0 7635 7792 8

Printed in China by Midas Printing (Asia) Ltd

Contents

CHAPTER 1

Firelight

"**K**ids who are sick need lots to drink," said Mom, coming into the bedroom with lemonade for Karlie.

Karlie propped herself up against the pillow, and sipped. "Please light the fire," she said. "*Please*, Mom."

"But the heat is on," said Mom. "It's nice and warm."

"I know," said Karlie. "But I want to see what this room was like for Victoria."

Mom laughed. "Victoria's parents built this house in 1880, when Victoria was three." She plumped the pillows. "A small fire isn't very warm in a big room with high ceilings — like this."

"Please, please, *please* light the fire," said Karlie. "If I'm going to solve mysteries, I have to know more about Victoria."

"All right," said Mom. "Just this once, especially for you."

Karlie hugged her. "Thanks, Mom."

Mom hurried away to get newspapers, matches, and firewood, and Karlie looked around, smiling.

Two months ago, Karlie's family had moved into this famous old stone house. Mom had a book describing it, and the different people who had lived there over the years.

Karlie's parents planned to renovate the house to be a bed-and-breakfast inn.

The real estate agent had said it was a house full of surprises and secrets. Karlie kept looking for a secret door, a secret staircase, and secret hiding places. For her, the house was still new, strange, and exciting.

The room that had been Victoria's bedroom would be used for guests, so Karlie was sleeping in it for only a few months. Soon her own small bedroom, which had been the maid's room, would be ready.

Mom came in with the things she needed for the fire. "It's getting dark—I'll switch on the light."

"No!" said Karlie. "Please don't! Victoria didn't have electric light."

Mom set the fire and lit it. The flames spread quickly. Karlie watched them flickering in the grate. The fire was captivating.

"There you are," said Mom as she walked toward the door. "Back to the 1880s."

"I'm pretending it's 1888," said Karlie. "Victoria is eleven, and so am I."

Gradually Karlie drifted off to sleep.

Thump!

Startled, Karlie sat up. "Just that silly old opossum," she said to herself.

Every evening, an opossum sprang from a branch of a big tree outside her window onto the roof, and scampered across it.

Wide awake now, Karlie looked around the room. In the firelight, everything had changed to soft glow and deep shadow. On the carved wooden panels around the fireplace, the leaves in each corner swooped toward an acorn in the center.

That acorn looks like a knob, Karlie thought.

CHAPTER 2

Secret Places

Karlie hopped out of bed and peered at the panel on the left. She tugged the acorn sideways and it moved a little.

It's stuck, she thought. No one has opened it for more than a hundred years.

At last the panel slid sideways.

"Ah!" said Karlie. "I think I've found Victoria's secret hiding place!"

She peered in and saw something—a square something—and then heard Mom on the stairs. Quickly, she closed the panel and slipped back into bed.

Mom came in. "How's the fire?"

"Beautiful," said Karlie. "Now I know how Victoria felt in her big, dark bedroom."

Mom kissed her and adjusted the quilt. "Go to sleep now. When Dad comes up to say goodnight, he'll take care of the fire."

The logs glowed and crumbled. Karlie waited.

After Dad says goodnight, I'll open the panel and...

When Karlie opened her eyes, it was morning. A memory flashed into her mind: I found Victoria's secret hiding place!

You'd never guess it was there, Karlie thought. The carving looks different in the daylight.

She hopped out of bed and opened the panel. Now she could see that the "square something" was a book with a red and green embossed cover.

She took it out and ran her fingers over the raised pattern, then sniffed the musty pages, going back in time to the 1880s.

Opening the book, she read:

⟿ Victoria's Diary ⟿

For our darling girl
on her 11th birthday,
October 19th, 1888,
with all our love,
Mama and Papa

Karlie heard someone on the stairs. Dad was bringing breakfast!

She put Victoria's diary back, closed the panel, and jumped into bed.

"Good morning," said Dad, coming in with a tray. "How are you feeling?"

"I'm much better," Karlie replied. "I'll get up soon."

Dad put the tray down on the bed, and plumped the pillows.

Looking at the food, Karlie realized how hungry she was. "Wow! Thanks, Dad!"

While she ate breakfast, she thought about her discovery. What had Victoria written?

When Karlie had finished eating, she hopped up, brought Victoria's diary back to bed, and opened it up to the first page.

CHAPTER 3

Secret Diary

October 19th, 1888

This diary from Mama and Papa is a splendid birthday surprise. I want to go down to the gatehouse now, and show it to Kate Riley, but I am not permitted. Kate, John, and Mary have scarlet fever, and Papa says they will infect me. I hope the little ones don't catch it. Hundreds of children have died of scarlet fever this year.

I shall keep my diary in my secret hiding place. No one will read it except me, but I shall

14

tell Kate about it. Kate and I have secrets, which we do not tell her three brothers and two sisters.

I cannot wait for my birthday dinner. It will be special. I am a fortunate girl, much more fortunate than the Riley children.

~

Mom came up for the tray.

"I found Victoria's secret hiding place," said Karlie, hopping out of bed. "Look! And here's her diary."

Mom read the first entry. "Oh," she said. "Scarlet fever. Hundreds of children died of scarlet fever and other diseases in those days."

"Why did they die?" Karlie asked.

"They didn't have modern medicine," said Mom. "Antibiotics hadn't been invented, so they couldn't kill the germs."

"Poor kids!" said Karlie.

"Kids are lucky today," said Mom. "When they're babies, their parents take them to be immunized so they don't get other diseases like measles, chickenpox, or whooping cough."

"Was I immunized?" Karlie asked.

"Yes, you'll never get those diseases," said Mom.

"I'm much better," said Karlie. "I want to get up today."

"This afternoon," said Mom. "Stay in bed and keep warm this morning. I'm going shopping soon."

Karlie climbed back into bed and opened Victoria's diary again. She read the next entry.

As it is my birthday, Mama said I may read my magazines, Cheerful Sundays: Stories and Poems for Children, *which I read only on Sundays. I would like to share them with Kate, but I am not permitted. Papa says that the Riley children would damage them.*

I shall take my treasures from my secret hiding place and play with them. Then I shall choose something to wear with my blue velvet dress at my birthday dinner. Shall I wear my bead necklace, or the cameo on the velvet band, or the gold bracelet? Mama will decide.

～

Victoria's treasures! thought Karlie. In another secret hiding place? She looked and saw that the pattern was the same on both sides of the fireplace.

Karlie grasped the acorn knob on the right and wriggled it until the panel slid open. Inside were two boxes, which she took back to bed.

CHAPTER 4

Secret Treasures

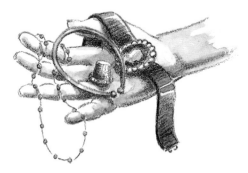

The first box was a leather one. Karlie jiggled the stiff catch until it opened.

One by one, she took out Victoria's treasures: a necklace of blue beads, a silver thimble, a cameo on a velvet band, and a gold bracelet.

She opened the second box—a cardboard one—and examined the treasures as she took them out: a cowrie shell, a feather, a tiny green bottle, a pale-blue bird's egg, and a strange white *something*.

"What is it?" she said to herself as she turned the curious object over. At last she knew. "A tiny skull—from a bird, perhaps, or a mouse?"

Carefully, Karlie put the treasures back into their boxes, and opened Victoria's diary once more.

～

My godfather, Sir Peter Pethrick from England, is coming to my special birthday dinner. It is always exciting when he comes. I wonder what he will bring? Mama says I must not expect anything, but he always brings a special gift.

～

I wonder what Victoria's godfather gave her, thought Karlie. I know! The silver thimble in her treasure box.

She put it on her finger. The silver had darkened with age. The grooves of the intricate pattern on the border were almost black.

"It needs a polish," she said.

She went downstairs into the laundry, opened the cabinet, and found some silver polish and a cloth.

When Mom came home, Karlie was rubbing the thimble. They went upstairs together, and Karlie showed Victoria's treasures to her mother.

"Oh, Karlie," said Mom, picking them up, one by one, and turning them over. "Aren't they lovely?"

After lunch, Karlie read Victoria's diary again.

~

October 20th, 1888

Last night I wore the cameo on the velvet band at my birthday dinner. I blew out the candles on my cake, and my godfather gave me a small box in crimson wrapping with gold ribbon. Inside was a leather pouch, and inside the pouch was a shiny new coin.

Tonight, in the moonlight, I shall slip out and hide it in my secret cave. Kate is the only person who knows my secret cave hiding place.

~

Not the thimble, thought Karlie. A coin. Victoria's godfather gave her a coin.

Where had Victoria hidden it? "Victoria's secret cave is a hiding place outside. Perhaps it's a real cave on the riverbank," she muttered to herself.

Mom was stripping paint off the banisters.

"May I go for a walk?" Karlie asked.

"Yes, dear," said Mom. "Just a little walk. Put a jacket on to keep warm."

Karlie walked down to the river. She stood and looked all along the steep bank. She walked farther, searching as she went, but she couldn't see a cave.

CHAPTER 5

Secret Hiding Place

Returning, Karlie opened Victoria's diary once more.

October 21st, 1888

When I woke, I felt very hot. Dr. Shaw came and examined me and diagnosed scarlet fever. I have to stay in bed and keep warm. I shall not see Kate Riley for many weeks.

I did not tell Mama about my adventure last night. I climbed out the window in my nightgown, crawled along the branch, and put my coin into my cave with my magazines.

The opossums had made a nest again, so I cleaned it out. When I am better I shall make a Keep Out sign!

I cannot stop shivering...

~

Karlie turned the pages, and was surprised to discover that Victoria hadn't written any more. She pulled the quilt up and snuggled into the warmth.

The next morning, Karlie looked at the branch from which the opossums leaped onto the roof.

Victoria's cave is a hollow in my big tree! How did Victoria climb across to the branch? It's too far, she thought.

After a moment, Karlie guessed. Back in 1888, the branch came close to the window. Someone sawed it off years ago. It's close enough for the opossums, but not for me.

Karlie went down to the garden shed and dragged a ladder to the tree. She climbed to the first branch and pulled herself up, up, until she reached the branch that stretched toward her bedroom.

Immediately, she saw Victoria's cave. It was filled with leaves and sticks. She searched, hoping to find Victoria's *Cheerful Sundays* magazines, but they had rotted away long ago.

Then Karlie saw a small hole, and she reached in. Feeling something firm, she tugged, pulled it out, and turned it over.

"It's a coin pouch."

As she lifted the flap, the leather pouch fell to pieces, and dropped into the nest.

"Oh, no!"

But in her hand was a heavy coin. She rubbed it on her jeans and soon it shone.

"It's the gift from Victoria's godfather!" Karlie exclaimed.

Quickly, she climbed down from branch to branch—slipping and clutching—and rushed inside.

"Mom!" said Karlie. "I found an old coin with a face and print and a date."

"It's not a British florin," said Mom. "Florins are silver. This is gold—perhaps it's a guinea." She looked closely. "It's a Queen Victoria gold sovereign from 1888. Where did you find it?"

Karlie told her about Victoria's cave.

"I found Victoria's birthday gift," said Karlie, skipping along the hall. "A sovereign—wow!"

I've found surprises and secrets, she thought. I knew I would, and now that I can imagine Victoria here, it's a very special house.